"LC"   "Cap"

ICE
SKATING
POND

For Ethan and Nate

HBJ

Harcourt Brace Jovanovich, Publishers
San Diego   New York   London

Mouse Writing

by Jim Arnosky

LIBRARY OF CONGRESS CATALOGING IN
PUBLICATION DATA
Arnosky, Jim.
Mouse writing.
Summary: A pair of skating mice trace out letters
of the cursive alphabet on the ice.
1. English language—Alphabet—Juvenile
literature. 2. Penmanship—Copy-books—
Juvenile literature.
[1. Alphabet. 2. Penmanship] I. Title
PE1155.A7 1983   421'.1   83-4298
ISBN 0-15-256028-9
Printed in the United States of America
First edition   B C D E

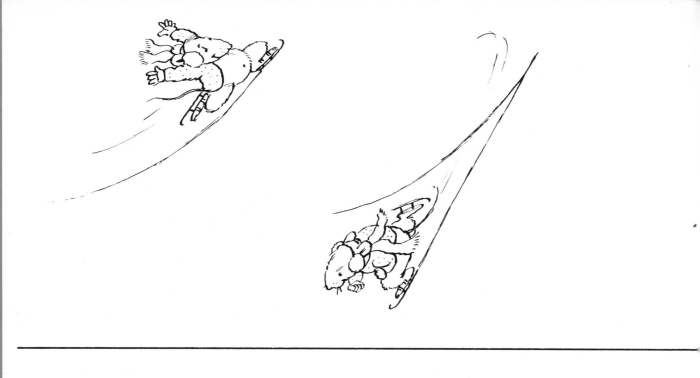

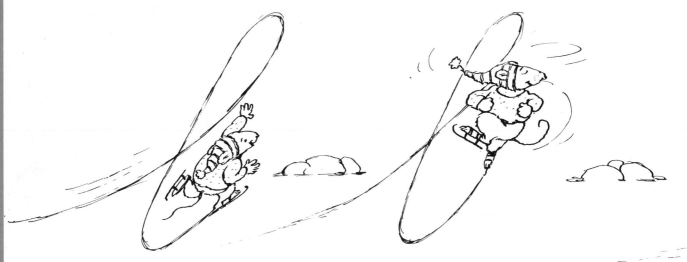

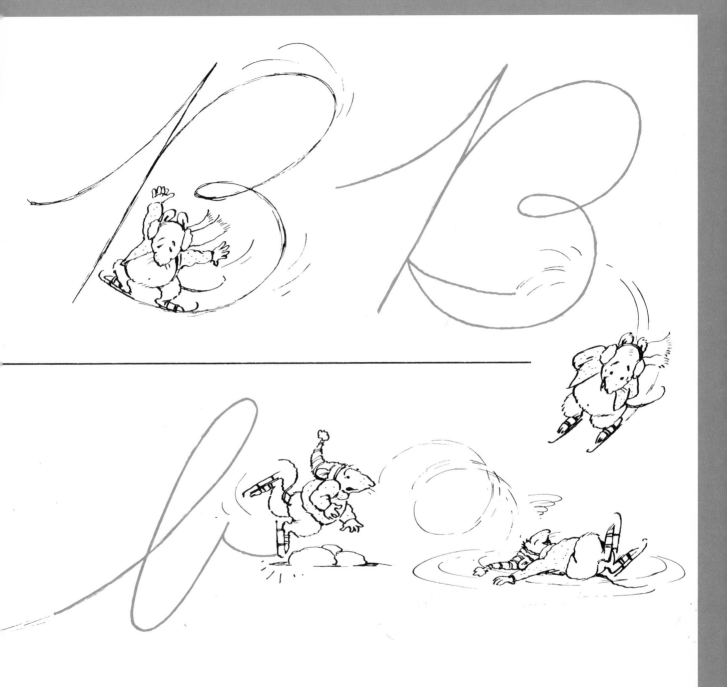